MR GUM

and the Power Crystals

'It provoked long and painful belly laughs from my daughter, who is eight.' Daily Telegraph

'As always, Stanton has a ball with dialogue, detail and devilish plot twists.' Scotsman

'We laughed so much it hurt.' Sophie, aged 9

'You will laugh so much you'll ache in places you didn't know you had.' First News

'A riotous read.' Sunday Express

'It's utterly bonkers and then a bit more - you'll love every madcap moment.' TBK Magazine

'Chaotically crazy.' Jewish Chronicle

'Designed to tickle young funny bones.' Glasgow Herald

'A complete joy to read whatever your age.' This is Kids' Stuff

'The truth is a lemon meringue!' Friday O'Leary

'They are brilliant.' Zoe Ball, Radio 2

'Smooky palooki! This book is well brilliant.' Jeremy Strong

'They're the funniest books . . . I can't recommend them enough.' Stephen Mangan

For Toby, all the way in New Zealand

DEAN

Mr Gum and the Power Crystals
First published 2006 by Egmont UK Limited
This edition published 2019 by Dean, an imprint of Egmont UK Limited,
The Yellow Building,1 Nicholas Road
London W11 4AN

Text copyright © 2006 Andy Stanton
Illustration copyright © 2006 David Tazzyman

The moral rights of the author and illustrator have been asserted

mrgum.co.uk
www.egmont.co.uk

A CIP catalogue record for this title is available from the British Library
Printed and bound in Great Britain by the CPI Group

70881/001

MR **GUM**

and the
Power Crystals

ANDY
STANTON

Illustrated by David Tazzyman

DEAN

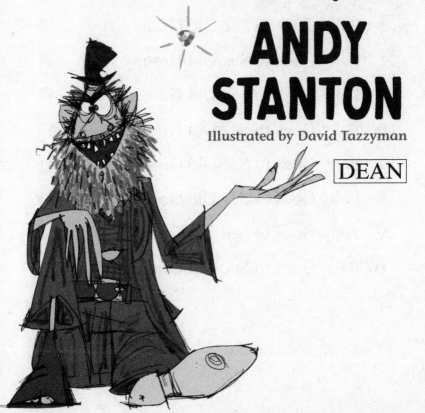

Contents

Some of the crazy old townsfolk from Lamonic Bibber

Mrs Lovely

Friday O'Leary

Billy William the Third

Old Granny

Mr Gum

Martin Launderette

Hey! How come I'm not in this story?

Alan Taylor

Polly

INTRODUCTION: Why do things Happen?

'Why do things happen?' That's the question on everyone's lips these days. 'Why do things happen, Science?' everyone's lips ask Science. And luckily, Science usually has the answer. For example, if you ask Science why your little sister is crying, the answer is plain – because you called her 'Stinky' and broke all her dolls with a hammer. Or if you ask Science why rain falls from the sky, the answer is simple – because it just does and stuff.

But every so often something happens which is so extraordinary that even Science does not hold the answers. For instance, take the horrifying events of last summer in the little town of Lamonic Bibber. 'Why did they happen, Science?' you may ask. But you will get no answer.

For some things are so strange that they cannot be explained away with Science. Or Maths. Or even P.E. But like Old Granny said as she rocked back and forth in her chair by the fireside:

'The past has a way of repeating itself. The past has a way of repeating itself. The past has a way of repeating itself.'

And perhaps that is all that anyone can say of such things.

Chapter 1
The Strange Stones

It all started one hot afternoon, down by the Lamonic River where the water rushes grow. A nine-year-old girl called Polly was skipping along by the water's edge and oh, what a happy little nibblehead she was! It was the height of summer and the world was her playground, sparkling with colour and excitement at every twist and turn.

FLINK! A trout leapt from the clear water in a flash of silver scales.

BZZZZ! A bumblebee did that thing where it goes really near your ear and makes you jump in astonishment.

WHOOOOOSH-THUMP-SQUISH! A kingfisher soared gracefully into the side of a sycamore tree, plummeted to the ground and was stepped on by an otter.

The warblers warbled and the dragonflies dragonflew and the frogs texted 'RIBBET' to each other on their mobiles. And the sun shone down upon them all as if to say, 'Here, have loads of heat off me for a laugh.' It was the height of summer all right.

'Oranges an' mermaids, says the bells of Saint Dickens!' sang Polly as she skip-skap-skappled along. 'I owe you five matchsticks, says the bells of –'

BARK!

Suddenly there came a sound from the Old Meadow yonder, a sound so happy that for one amazing moment all the soldiers in the world put down their guns and did a bit of hopscotch instead.

BAAARK!

There it was again, even happier than before and with a couple of extra 'A's in the middle free of charge.

'SPARKLERS!' shouted Polly joyously. 'It's Jake, the Number One Best Woofdog on the Woofdog Charts, an' that's a official Polly Fact!'

Crashing through the undergrowth she followed the barking to the Old Meadow yonder, and yes! There was big Jake himself, doing what he loved best – digging an enormous hole with his legendary paws. Dirt was flyin', flies were buzzin', cows were mooin', letter 'g's' were missin' – it was chaos.

'Hey, Jakey, let me play too!' laughed Polly, running over. But even as she spoke Jake was emerging from the hole, a small brown object clutched between his doggy-go-lucky teeth.

'What you found, what you found?' said Polly, petting the energetic beast until he gobbed the thing proudly into the long grass. It was a little bag made of rough cloth and tied with red ribbon. Here and there it had been nibbled away by insects and pumpkins, but the material was thick and had withstood even the greediest attacks.

'What's that?' said Polly, squinting at something written on the bag, scratched into the cloth in rusty red ink:

1559

'Ooh,' she marvelled. 'This bag must be

from them long-ago Olden Days what's written in the history books. An' it's probbly a-burstin' with buried treasures what no one's never seen for thousands of years!'

With trembling fingers Polly untied the ribbon. Then, hardly daring to breathe, she tipped the contents of the bag into her sweaty palm.

'Smooky palooki!' she sighed. 'These things is well beautiful!'

For she was holding two strangely shaped stones, one pink and one white, glinting in the bright sunshine, glinting more brightly than anything Polly had ever seen before. They were beautiful indeed – and yet, Polly thought, there was something strange about their beauty. It was a cold, evil kind of beauty that would destroy you if you got too close, like a beautiful goose standing on a hillside.

You walk towards the goose, transfixed by its beauty. You want to touch the goose! You want to feel its soft feathery back and maybe have a cheeky stroke of its neck. But it is only when you are up close that you realise it is not a goose at all, but a cruel wolf with hunger in his eyes and a plastic beak strapped to his face.

Yet try as she might, Polly could not tear her eyes away. The stones were so beautiful. She wanted

HONK,
GRRR

to look at them forever, or slightly longer if possible. They made her feel strong, as if she could achieve anything . . .

By her side Jake gave a little whimper, and Polly looked up, startled from her daydreams.

'Oh,' she laughed uneasily. 'Look how dark it's got while I been a-starin' at these stones! I done lost track of the times!'

And so, putting the stones in her pocket, Polly headed for home. The sun was setting and the shadows were creeping out to play and she found herself walking slightly faster than normal.

'Not cos I'm scared or nothin',' she told Jake. 'Jus' cos I wanna see what it's like walkin' fast, that's all.'

But as they walked, Polly had the feeling that unfriendly eyes were upon her. And she was very glad indeed when they were finally away from the riverside and heading back into town.

'These stones are brilliant,' she told herself later that evening. But all the same, she locked them safely away in her jewellery box before she went to bed.

'Not cos I'm frightened of them or nothin',' she told herself. 'Jus' cos I wanna see what it's like putting things in my jewellery box, that's all.'

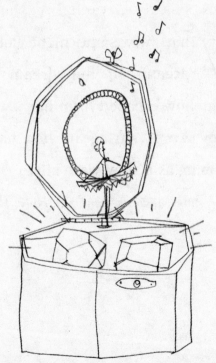

Chapter 2

Polly's Bad Dream

That very same night Polly had a strange dream. In her dream the stones had somehow escaped from her jewellery box. There they were, sitting in her hand, turning and moving as if they were alive.

Take us to the windmill, Polly, the stones seemed

to whisper inside her head. *Take us to the windmill!*

'But there aren't no windmills in Lamonic Bibber,' Polly frowned sleepily. 'You only gets windmills in foreign countries like Indostralia an' the United States of Wales, don't you?'

Take us to the windmill, the stones seemed to whisper again. *It is our Destiny.*

'No,' said Polly, more firmly this time. 'It's jus' my imaginations an' I'm not a-listenin'!'

Awww, go on, take us, said the pink one.

It'll be a laugh.

We'd take YOU to the windmill if YOU wanted to go, said the white one.

'For the last time, NO!' cried Polly in her dream. But unable to help herself, she was getting up anyway. She was getting up and opening her bedroom door. Now she was standing in the bathroom brushing her teeth . . .

No time for dental hygiene, whispered the stones. *Take us to the windmill!*

'Honestly,' said Polly crossly. 'Don't you two ever think 'bout nothin' but a-goin' to windmills?'

Not really, whispered the stones. *It is our Destiny.*

'Well, it's my Destiny to go back to bed right now an' dream of friendly ponies instead,' replied Polly. But even as she said this she was gazing at the stones as if entranced, thinking how pretty they looked . . .

And before she knew it she was out the front door and underneath the stars. It was very late.

Not a soul saw her as she made her way down to the river, gliding along soundlessly in her bare feet. High above the moon shone like a silver coin from the Olden Days, and glancing up, Polly saw a dreadful thing – for the moon was changing, changing before her very eyes.

Round and round whizzed the moon's silvery disc . . . Now it seemed like the sails of a great windmill, turning and turning in the sky above . . . And now it changed to become a huge loaf of

freshly baked bread . . . But then the bread was burning, burning, until it was nothing more than cinders and ashes . . . And then it changed once more to become a face that Polly knew only too well. A horrifying face with a big red beard, a face with two angry bloodshot eyes . . .

'Mr Gum!' Polly cried out. 'What's that beardy old criminal doin' here? Even in dreams, he is the worst!'

But then the awful vision was gone and the

moon was just the moon again. Except it still had
a bit of Mr Gum's beard on by accident. And part
of his nose.

🐽 🐽 🐽

'I don't like this dream,' said Polly as she walked
along. The warm wind ruffled her pyjamas and
the grass swished secretly at her feet. 'I wants to
wake up,' she whimpered. 'I really truly does.'

But the stones in her hand had other ideas.

Keep walking, Polly, they whispered softly. *We're nearly there.*

And how could Polly resist? Those stones were so pretty, so pretty in the moonlight . . .

On she went. In the Old Meadow a field mouse swooped down and carried off a barn owl in its sharp claws. A fox prowled slyly through the hedgerows selling cheap lighters and stolen DVDs. A badger slid past, brushing lightly against Polly's ankle. But Polly noticed nothing except the stones in her hand, pulsing softly with an eerie pink–white light.

But where was that light leading her? Further along the Lamonic River she went and further still, further than the children of the town were ever allowed to venture. Until rounding a wide bend in the riverbank, Polly came upon a place she had never before seen. Here the bushes grew thick and wild. Here the trees crowded gloomily overhead. And here, half-hidden among

the weeds was a rickety wooden bridge like the one in that famous fairy tale, *The Troll Who Wanted To Eat Some Goats*. A rickety wooden bridge that led across the water towards –

'A windmill,' whispered Polly in fascination. 'There really is a windmill in Lamonic Bibber!'

Yes, there it stood, silhouetted against the starry velvet night. Perhaps it had once been a jolly sight, pointing towards the sky like a lovely wooden ice cream as children and tulips danced around it doing their games. But no longer. Its red paint was peeling and faded. The wooden boards

had rotted away in places, leaving dark gaping holes where I bet you anything there were rats. And the whole thing leaned lopsidedly towards the river, as if beckoning Polly to come closer. But Polly didn't want to come closer. The more she stared at the windmill the less she liked it.

Over the bridge now, Polly! the stones whispered eagerly. *Just a few more steps and then we'll be there!*

'No way, things of clay!' Polly told them with as much strength as she could muster.

'I'm not a-goin' anywhere near that old spooker, so unlucky, you lose! I'm a-goin' homes right now!'

But you know what dreams are like – sometimes you just can't control your own two feet, or your own zero feet if you are dreaming about being a snake. Before she knew it, Polly was gliding across the rickety wooden bridge, straight for the windmill. Its broken doorway gaped darkly ahead, as if it wished to swallow her up for a

midnight feast.

And then Polly saw the most awful thing of all . . .

Because high up in that windmill a face appeared at the window, a face that Polly knew only too well. A horrifying face with a big red beard, a face with two angry bloodshot eyes . . .

'MR GUM AGAIN!' shrieked Polly in utter terror. 'IT'S MR GUM AN' THAT CAN'T MEAN

NOTHIN' BUT EVILS!'

But her feet were still moving forward. With mounting horror she felt herself take a step towards the windmill. Then another.

Then another.

☾ ☾ ☾

'NOOOOOO!' cried Polly, starting awake. Her heart was pounding and for one frightful moment she thought she was in the windmill's building-y clutches – but no. She was lying in her own bed, safe as a rectangle.

'Thank the Forces of Good,' she panted. 'It was all just a bad dreamer what wasn't real whatsonever, so shut up if you say it was!'

But that's when Polly saw that she was holding the stones in her hand.

'No,' she moaned. 'No, it can't be! I locked 'em up in my jewellery box 'fore I wents to bed!'

Trembling, she threw back the covers – and

there was all the evidence she needed. Her bare feet were filthy with grass and mud from the riverside. Her ankle smelt like a badger. And she was wearing a souvenir T-shirt she'd never seen before:

I WENT TO THE

WINDMILL
IN MY SLEEP
AND ALL I GOT WAS
THIS LOUSY T-SHIRT!

'So it wasn't no proper normal nightmare after all,' said Polly thoughtfully as dawn crept across the sky outside her window. 'There's some peculiar stuff a-goin' on round here, an' I intends to get to the bottom of it or my name's not Jammy Grammy Lammy F'Huppa F'Huppa Berlin Stereo Eo Eo Lebb C'Yepp Nermonica Le Straypek De Grespin De Crespin De Spespin De Vespin De Whoop De Loop De Brunkle Merry Christmas Lenoir!'

Chapter 3

Polly Goes to See Old Granny

Later that morning Polly was eating a bowl of her favourite breakfast cereal, 'Baron von Tubblewobble's *Crunchy Little Leopards*'. Good golly, Miss Molly, she was tired! She'd spent half the night watching the stones to make sure they didn't get up to any more of their tricks. There they sat now on the kitchen table, one pink, one white, but both of them evil through and through. Polly was quite sure of it.

'Oh, I does wish Friday O'Leary was here,'

she yawned. 'He'd know just what to do. But he's off in Spainland on his honeymoonin's with Mrs Lovely.'

Yes, it was true. With Friday away there was no one that Polly could turn to for help. No one, that is, except –

Suddenly she jumped up from her seat like a lucky pineapple who's just won the National Lottery.

'OLD GRANNY!' cried Polly, spitting a mouthful of *Crunchy Little Leopards* all over the kitchen floor in her excitement. 'She's been alive for ages, nearly forever in fact! She's bound to know stuff 'bout mysterious no-good stones from the Olden Days!'

'We're free!' laughed the **Crunchy Little Leopards**, even though they were only made of wheat. And out the front door they ran.

🪟 🪟 🪟

Well, Polly didn't waste another moment. Packing the stones into their little bag, she set off for Old Granny's house immediately. It was a beautiful morning and with each step she took, Polly's bad dream seemed less and less real.

The sun smiled down upon her, the squirrels waved their little paws as she passed and a postman was attacked by hundreds of **Crunchy Little Leopards** who pounced on him and ran off down the road with his hat.

'Ah,' said Polly. 'Everythin's back to normal. An' here I am at last at Old Granny's house. But that's funny,' she frowned, taking a closer look. 'This doesn't look nothin' like Old Granny's

house. For a start, it's a lot more river-y. An'
also I can't help but notice there's a tumbledown
windmill here instead of Old Granny's house.'

Oops! the stones seemed to whisper
innocently. *We must have led you in totally the wrong
direction and come to the windmill by mistake. Oh, well. Now
we're here, we may as well go inside.*

And then Polly realised that the stones had
done it again, even when she was awake! They
definitely had strange powers – and they were

growing stronger all the time. And even worse, the windmill was still there. It wasn't just in dreams. There it was, just as real as you or me, especially me.

'Stones, you are the worst little crafters what I ever met!' scolded Polly. 'You done tricked me into comin' here an' I hates your spooky windmill, I hates it!'

And with a mighty effort of will, she turned around and started back towards town.

Chapter 4
Polly Goes to See Old Granny

As soon as Polly started back towards town, the stones seemed to cry out louder than ever inside her head.

Hey, said the pink stone. *I've just had a great idea.*

Let's all turn around and go back to the windmill!

Yes, let's! said the white stone. *Turn around, turn around, Polly!*

'N-no,' said Polly, trying to ignore their persistent whispers. It was so tempting to give in to all that hassling. 'But no!' she gasped as she marched determinedly along. 'I'm not the kinds of girl who allows herself to be bossed 'round by a couple of stones! I'm a-goin' to see Old Granny – an' that's final!'

On she marched, and very soon there she

was – crossing the rickety wooden bridge that led to . . .

the windmill.

'OH, MARZIPAN!' exclaimed Polly. 'THIS IS GETTIN' WELL ANNOYIN'!'

oh, marzipan –

Chapter 5

Polly Goes to See
Old Granny

Somehow Polly managed to turn away from the windmill. Every step was more difficult than the last, and even the first one was quite hard so just think about it. But she kept on going, back over the rickety wooden bridge and towards town. And eventually, after a GIGANTIC effort, she had finally made it. There she was – crossing the rickety wooden bridge that led to the windmill.

'OH, MARZIPAN!' exclaimed Polly. And turning away from the windmill yet again, she headed over the rickety wooden bridge back towards town. And eventually there she was . . .

oh, marzipan –

Chapter 6

Polly Goes to See Old Granny

. . . back at the windmill.

'OH, MARZIPAN!' exclaimed Polly. And turning away from the windmill yet again, she headed back over the rickety wooden bridge towards town. And eventually there she was . . .

Oh, marzipan –

Chapter 7

Polly Goes to See Old Granny

. . . back at the windmill.

'OH, MARZIPAN!' exclaimed Polly. And turning away from the windmill yet again, she headed back over the rickety wooden bridge towards town. And eventually there she was . . .

Oh, marzipan —

Chapter 8

Polly Goes to See Old Granny

. . . back at the windmill.

'OH, MARZIPAN!' exclaimed Polly. And turning away from the windmill yet again, she headed back over the rickety wooden bridge towards town. And eventually there she was . . .

Oh, marzipan —

Chapter 9

Polly Goes to See Old Granny

. . . back at the windmill.

'OH, MARZIPAN!' exclaimed Polly. And turning away from the windmill yet again, she headed back over the rickety wooden bridge towards town. And eventually there she was . . .

Oh, low fat yoghurt—

Chapter 10

Polly Goes to See Old Granny

. . . back at the windmill.

'OH, LOW FAT YOGHURT!' exclaimed Polly, just to see if anyone was still paying attention. And turning away from the windmill yet again, she headed back over the rickety wooden bridge towards town. And eventually there she was . . .

Oh, marzipan —

Chapter 11

Polly Goes to See Old Granny

. . . back at the windmill.

'OH, MARZIPAN!' exclaimed Polly. And turning away from the windmill yet again, she headed back over the rickety wooden bridge towards town. And eventually there she was . . .

Oh, marzipan —

Chapter 12
What Happened at the Windmill

. . . back at the windmill.

'OH, MARZIPAN!' exclaimed Polly in frustration. But before she could turn back towards the town, there came a rustling sound as a battered old hobnail boot appeared from among the bushes.

But wait, there was more. The hobnail boot led to a hobnail sock. The hobnail sock led to dirty, raggedy trousers like a tramp would wear. The trousers led to a shabby jacket too disgraceful even for a tramp. The jacket led to a scruffy red beard. The beard led to two angry bloodshot eyes and the bloodshot eyes led to the truth of who it was climbing from those bushes:

Why, it was Oliver J. Chestnuts, the friendliest, funniest old fellow in the whole wide world!

No, not really.

In actual fact it was Mr Gum.

And he was scowling like a fireplace.

♪ ♪ ♪

For a long moment Mr Gum and Polly simply stood there, facing each other in the fading afternoon light. Neither the old man nor the little girl said a word but in that moment each understood they

were the exact opposite of each other. The two of
them were natural enemies, like a spider and a fly.
Or a cat and a mouse. Or an eagle and something
that doesn't like eagles very much.

'So, you little meddler,' scowled Mr Gum
eventually. 'You found them strange stones what
I been searchin' for in the windmill all this time.'

'Then it *was* you I saw nosin' around here last
night in my sort-of-dream-type-thing,' said Polly.

'Yeah, probably,' agreed Mr Gum. 'Cos I

know the power what lives inside them stones. An' I know you can feel it too, can't ya?' he continued slyly, inching towards Polly in his hobnail boots.

'No,' said Polly, but she was shaking all over. Mr Gum was right – she could feel the power, growing stronger by the second.

'Give in, little girl,' murmured Mr Gum, coming closer still. 'Give in an' join forces with me!'

'No way!' said Polly, but her voice was

unsteady. The stones felt very heavy and hot in her hand and it was hard to think straight . . .

'Give in,' wheedled Mr Gum. 'Together we'll take them stones up into the windmill, an' then jus' imagine how powerful we'll be!'

'No, Mr Gum, I'm not like you,' gasped Polly weakly, but the stones were whispering, whispering worse than ever.

Give in to Mr Gum and you can have anything you want! they whispered. *Anything at all!*

And now the stones were showing Polly things, filling her head with visions of incredible power . . .

She saw herself as an Evil Queen, powerful and tall, with a robe and everything. The world was hers to command.

She had only to lift a hand and mountains would crumble into the sea . . . She had only to raise a finger and cities would crumble into the sea . . . She had only to say a word and forests would crumble into the sea . . .

Basically she could make things crumble into the sea if she fancied, that's how powerful she was.

'Ha ha!' she laughed. 'I am Evil Queen Polly an' I've a-given in to the Bad Side an' Mr Gum's my new best friend an' we spend all our time makin' things crumble into the sea an' watchin' "Bag of Sticks" on the world's biggest TV screen. Ha ha ha!'

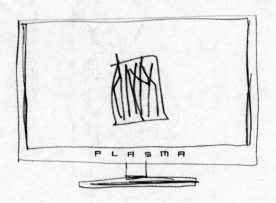

'BUT NO, YOU EVILLERS!' roared Polly, shaking her head like crazy to clear these appalling thoughts from her mind. 'I won't never go over to no Bad Side so get lost, plain an' simple!'

'Shabba me whiskers!' yelled Mr Gum furiously. 'How can you resist me temptin' offer, little girl?'

'It's called believin' in the Forces of Good!' cried Polly just as furiously as he. 'An' it's somethin' you wouldn't know nothin' about, you cucumber!'

'Oh, BLEM!' shouted Mr Gum, losing the last of his patience and lunging for the stones. 'Jus' gimme them things! I wants to take 'em to the windmill an' I wants to take 'em now! An' I'm not a cucumber – *you* are!'

And with that it was **CHASING TIME!**

Chapter 13
Chasing Time!

Yes, it was ***CHASING TIME!*** and it had everything you need for a good chase, including:

- A Person Running Away running away
- A Chasing Guy chasing after them
- A few trees
- A river

🐛 A bit where the Person Running Away trips over and the Chasing Guy laughs but then he's so busy laughing he skids into the river and a newt swims up his nose

🐚 Some pebbles

🐚 Some more pebbles

🍃 A leaf

Oh, it was **CHASING TIME!** all right, no doubt about it.

The Person Running Away (Polly) felt as if she had been running away forever. Her legs were going all shaky and useless. Surely the Chasing Guy (Mr Gum) must have given up by now? But no. She could hear him galloping after her in his hobnail boots, always just a few steps behind. So on she ran, and the riverside animals watched and prayed that she would escape from that terrible individual.

Come on, Polly! the otters seemed to nod with their wise, whiskery faces.

You can do it, you nine-year-old champion! the woodpeckers seemed to tap, high up in the treetops.

We don't really care what happens, buzzed the wasps. *If anything we're probably on Mr*

Gum's side, to be honest.

And that proves it once and for all: wasps are truly the roo-de-lallies of the insect kingdom.

But now, perhaps spurred on by those very wasps, the Chasing Guy was getting closer to the

Person Running Away. Polly could feel horrible hot breath upon her neck, and glancing over her shoulder Mr Gum's yibbering face seemed to fill the entire world. His bloodshot eyes were alight with anger. His mouth hung open as dark as the doorway to the windmill itself. His big red beard flipped and flapped as he ran. And perhaps most

upsetting of all – there was a newt hanging out of his left nostril.

'Gimme them things!' shouted Mr Gum, and Polly felt sharp fingernails rake against her back, tearing at her dress. Panting with exhaustion, she ducked under an archway of prickly brambles and turned from the riverbank

to plunge into the woods beyond. Hither and thither she ran, through the dark confusion of the trees, but Mr Gum was always just a few steps behind. It looked hopeless.

And then up ahead, Polly saw a shadowy figure emerging from a gooseberry bush.

'Mister, won't you a-helps me?' she cried wildly. But even as she spoke a filthy stale stench wafted her way and she knew she was done for.

For it was none other than England's Most Revolting Butcher, Billy William the Third.

'Oh, I'll "a-helps" you, all right,' cackled Billy William, grinning so nastily that he should have been sent to prison for just that facial expression alone. 'I'll a-helps you get them power crystals to the windmill where they belong!'

Power crystals?! Polly had time to think – but all the while she was talking to Billy, Mr Gum was snurfling up behind her, silent as a carpet.

What a master of snurfling that man was! He even had a *Certificate of Snurfling* on his kitchen wall. He had stolen it from the *University of Snurfling* by snurfling up to their window ledge and grabbing it when no one was looking.

Slowly, like a pair of horrifying toenails, Mr Gum and Billy closed in, trapping Polly against the broad trunk of an ancient oak tree. And now it wasn't just Mr Gum who was snurfling up on her. Billy had joined in too.

Snurfle. Billy snurfled up on the left.

Snurfle. Mr Gum snurfled up on the right.

Snurfle. Billy snurfled up on the left.

Snurfle. Mr Gum snurfled up on the right.

Snood. Billy tried a bit of snooding, just for a change.

Snurfle. Mr Gum stuck to the snurfles.

And finally, after all that snurfling (and the occasional snood), the villains were ready to pounce.

'Give us them stones, little girl,' growled Mr Gum. 'Pounce, Billy! Pounce, Billy! Pounce pounce pounce!'

But just as those villains pounced, a doorway hidden in the trunk of the tree swung open. Quick as an onion, a bony hand reached out, snatched up Polly and pulled her into the tree – and the only thing Billy and Mr Gum ended up grabbing was each other's

END OF CHAPTER 13

Chapter 14
Inside the Tree

*I*t was dark inside the oak tree, dark as night it was, and Polly had never been more scared in her whole life. OK, she had escaped all the snurfling – but for what? Something even worse, no doubt. The words of the famous proverb popped into her head:

Out of the snurfling pan,
into the ancient oak tree.

Never had those words seemed so true as they did now. All of a sudden the bony hand holding her arm gave a sharp squeeze and Polly let out a little scream.

What was going on?

What was to become of Polly at the bony hands of the bony-handed stranger?

And what was that sickly-sweet smell in the air?

It almost smelt like . . .

'Sherry,' whispered Polly. 'Old Granny, is that you?'

'Aye, young 'un, it is,' came the welcome reply.

'Oh, thank the Forces of Good!' wept Polly in relief, burying her face in Old Granny's petticoats and bashing her forehead on the bottle of sherry hidden amongst their folds.

'I been through terrible things, Old Granny! Terrible things indeeds!' she sobbed. 'An' Friday's off in Spainland an' I been tryin' to find you, Old Granny, an' there's bad mysteries goin' on, bad mysteries like I doesn't knows what!'

'Dry your eyes, young 'un,' soothed Old Granny, stroking Polly's hair with her bony hands. 'You are safe for now. By the way, sorry about my hands. I know they're a bit bony but they're the only ones I've got. Now come with me.'

And switching on her old-fashioned torch from before the War, Old Granny led the way down a spiral staircase carved into the very earth itself. How long did they walk down those stairs? No one can say, for time passes strangely when you are underground and it's quite dark and things. Down and down they went, only stopping now and then for Old Granny to take a sip of sherry from the bottle she always kept in her walking-stick. Down and down, until presently the steps levelled out and they found themselves at the entrance to a long narrow tunnel hardly higher than Polly's head. Beetles and millipedes scurried along the floor and tree roots poked through the earthen ceiling, dry and twisted and gnarled.

'Hmmph,' grunted Old Granny, breaking off one of the tree roots and eating it.

'How do you knows which ones is good to eat an' which ones is poisoners?' asked Polly in fascination.

'It is the Old Ways, young 'un,' said Old Granny, who was quite drunk. Secretly she spat out the disgusting-tasting tree root into her handkerchief before continuing. 'Most of this ancient wisdom is forgotten now, but us old folk still know the tricks.'

'Like this tunnel?' asked Polly.

'Aye,' said Old Granny, nodding slowly. 'These tunnels run under the whole of Lamonic

Bibber. My mother told me about them when I was just a little girl. "Old Granny," she told me. "There are some tunnels." My mother was a wonderful woman,' sighed Old Granny, wiping a tear from her eye. 'It was a shame the way those pelicans got her. But enough! We are here.'

The tunnel had been climbing steadily uphill for some time, and now in the dim torchlight Polly could see a small white door up ahead, half-overgrown with moss. What was

hidden behind that door? Polly dared not guess, but Old Granny pushed it back on its hinges and crawled through without a moment's thought. And following, Polly was amazed to find herself surrounded by bowls of boiled eggs with cling film over the top and a jar of piccalilli from before the War. The tunnel had come out in Old Granny's fridge.

'That's the way, young 'un,' said Old Granny, helping Polly out into the kitchen. 'Now come and sit by the fireside while Old Granny tells you her incredible tale.'

So Polly knelt down at the hearth and Old Granny lit the fire against the cold wind that had caught up outside.

'There,' said the old woman, 'a good old-fashioned blaze-up, that's the way.'

Old Granny stirred the fire with a poker.

Then she poured a few drops of sherry on to the flames, causing them to flicker and dance with a strange purplish light.

For some time she sat gazing with a faraway look into the flames, as if seeing pictures there from days long gone. She nodded occasionally and sipped her sherry and once Polly heard her gasp, 'Don't go in there, Mother! It's full of pelicans!' But eventually Old Granny seemed to remember where she was.

'Young 'un,' said she, turning to Polly. 'Show me what that whopper dog did find down by the Lamonic River where the water rushes grow.'

With a grimace, Polly took the coloured stones from her skirt pocket. She could not believe she had once thought them beautiful like a goose on a hill. They had brought nothing but trouble and now she could barely bear to bear them in her bare hands.

'Billy William called 'em power crystals,' whispered Polly as she placed them in Old Granny's withered palm.

'Aye,' nodded the old woman sadly, studying the wretched things in the firelight. 'And he was right.'

'What are they, Old Granny? What do they do?'

'I will tell you, young 'un,' replied the knowledgeable old drunkard. 'But it is a terrible business, it is a terrible business. Aye,' she added. 'It is a terrible business. A terri–'

'Excuse me, old 'un,' interrupted Polly politely. 'Are you a-gonna tell me 'bout it or are you jus' gonna keep on sayin' "it is a terrible business" over an' over?'

'Just a couple more,' said Old Granny. 'If that's all right with you.'

'Fair enough,' said Polly.

'It is a terrible business,' said Old Granny.

'Aye, a terrible business.'

And rocking back in her chair she began to tell her tale.

Chapter 15

Old Granny Tells Her Tale

'It was 1529,' Old Granny began, 'and it was totally rubbish. There was no TV, no rap music, no nothing. The King was a skinny old hunchback with no teeth, the Queen was an ant, and there was nothing to eat in the entire kingdom except for one enormous apple surrounded by the royal guards. I tell you, the Olden Days were a total waste of time.

"'I'm sick of it," said Nicholas de Twinklecakes one Wednesday morning, just after a delicious breakfast of nothing at all. "I haven't eaten for about a year and I'm starting to get hungry. I'm going to build a windmill, and then we can make loaves of bread."

"'Hoorah," said his wife and son. "Hoorah hoorah hoorah."

'So Nicholas worked hard to build his windmill,' continued Old Granny. 'He already had 3p, which made him the richest man in Lamonic Bibber at that time. Plus he found 2p under a piece of dirt and another 1p inside a dead peasant. That gave him 6p – more than enough to build a mighty windmill in those days.

'So he set to building and very soon it was done. There the windmill stood, on the banks of the Lamonic River, its heavy wooden sails turning just as fine as fine can be. And sure enough Nicholas and his family were soon feasting on loaves of bread every day.

'"Hoorah," said his wife and son. "Hoorah hoorah hoorah."'

'But the hoorahs didn't last long, young 'un. It was Midsummer's Eve when a fierce storm came a-calling. And just at that moment Nicholas' wife and son were standing under the windmill singing a song called "Hoorah. Hoorah hoorah hoorah."

'They had just reached the chorus when – FIZZ-FIZZ-OUCH! – they were struck by lightning. When Nicholas returned later that night he found them both dead. And what's more, the windmill was broken, for the storm had destroyed the machinery that made the sails go round.

'Then a dark look did come over Nicholas' face,' said Old Granny, taking a long sip of sherry. 'A dark look, even darker than the thunderous skies above. And as Nicholas knelt there by the riverside with an earthworm licking his shoe, he shouted, "I hate everything now! I've gone all bad and I'm going to destroy Lamonic Bibber with a huge cannon! No, wait, I've just had a better idea! I'm going to destroy it with power crystals instead! And the power crystals will make the sails of the windmill turn once more, but this time the windmill will not make loaves of bread. No, it will make PURE EVIL!"

'And then Nicholas de Twinklecakes uttered his famous curse –

"When next the windmill's sails do turn, Lamonic Bibber will burn and burn!"'

'But Old Granny, why would he want to burn

down the whole town into cinders an' ash?'
asked Polly. 'It doesn't make no senses!'

'It was grief for his dead wife and son,'
said Old Granny gently, rocking
back and forth in her chair
and farting all the while.
(Luckily the creaking of
the chair covered the
noise, and they
didn't smell too
much so she
just about got
away with it.)

'Yes, Nicholas' grief rose up inside his heart and drove him mad,' she continued sadly, 'and in his madness, he blamed the whole town for what had happened to his family.

'And so for the next thirty years no one saw Nicholas de Twinklecakes. Up there in his windmill he sat, all alone like a piece of old cheese that no one wants to dance with. His hair grew long and his face grew bitter and his arms sort of stayed about the same, but never mind.

He was busy with his experiments. Strange, unnatural experiments involving power and crystals. And eventually, after thirty years of toil, struggle and hardly combing his hair, he had finally done it. The year was 1559 –'

'Jus' like what it's written on the bag Jake found,' whispered Polly in the flickering firelight.

'It was 1559,' continued Old Granny, 'and it was Midsummer's Eve once more.

'"Ha ha!" crowed Nicholas from high up in

his windmill. "I have finally made some power crystals! And now to do that curse I mentioned earlier, about thirty years ago." Giggling madly, he ripped up a couple of floorboards and made them into a Power Crystal Control Panel.

'"Ha ha!" crowed Nicholas. "Now to put the crystals into the Control Panel – and it's burning time!"

'But at that moment there came a shout from below and peering down, Nicholas saw the townsfolk gathered around the windmill, brandishing flaming torches and chickens.

"We know what you're up to!" shouted the townsfolk. "We are going to get you, Nicholas de Twinklecakes!"

"'Oh, no!" cried Nicholas. "I haven't got time to put the power crystals in the Control Panel. I'd better run away."

'So Nicholas climbed out the back window and away he ran, over the fields and meadows, stopping only to bury the power crystals deep in the ground. Maybe he thought he'd get another chance to use them some other time – but it was not to be. Three days later he was found in a ditch, dead as a kettle and completely bald. He had been murdered by hair thieves.

'And that's how I heard the tale, as it has passed down from generation to generation,' finished Old Granny. 'To be honest, I made up the bit about the enormous apple but the rest of it is probably true. And I tell you, young 'un, ever since that time the windmill's sails have never once turned, not even in the strongest winds.'

Chapter 16

Attack of the Roo-de-lallies

'What a brilliant story that was,' said Polly after Old Granny was done. Outside the wind was howling and the first drops of rain were beginning to fall, a cold, cold rain that meant no one any good. 'The bad guy lost an' the townsfolk won an' all's well that ends well. Good night an' sweet dreams, says I!'

'Oh, young 'un,' said Old Granny. 'The story is not yet over, don't you see? Nicholas' chance has come again after all.'

'But all that stuff done happened ages ago!' exclaimed Polly. 'Nicholas de Twinklecakes is dead an' gone, you saids it yourself with your very own cracked old lips. It's all in the past!'

'Aye, young 'un,' said Old Granny mysteriously. 'But the past has a way of repeating itself. The past has a way of repeating itself. The past has a way of repeating itself. And the crystals are growing strong with power again. Tonight is Midsummer's Eve, and I dread to think what may happen if the crystals are taken to the windmill on a night like this.'

'Well, bad luck, you stupid old hassler, cos that's exactly where we're takin' them,' rasped a filthy voice, and spinning around Polly gasped to see Mr Gum and Billy William climbing from Old Granny's fridge, eating boiled eggs as they came. The roo-de-lallies had tracked them down!

'Yeah, that's right,' laughed Mr Gum, spitting bits of egg all over Old Granny's kitchen floor ON PURPOSE. 'We know all about that curse an' it sounds like a right laugh. An' now we're off to make it come true!'

'An' you're comin' with us,' Billy William told Polly, lassoing her with a rope of cow's intestines. 'You're gonna watch as your beloved

Lamonic Bibber burns, burns, burns!'

But no one had reckoned on Old Granny, perhaps not even Old Granny herself. Rising unsteadily from her rocking chair she turned to address the villains.

'**By the Forces of Good and the Power of Low-Price Sherry,**' cried Old Granny in an amazing strong voice completely different from her usual worn-out croaking, '**I command thee foul roo-de-lallies be gone from this house!**'

And in that moment, Old Granny no longer looked like a shrivelled-up wrinkler with strange brown spots all over her hands and a bit of a moustache when you looked up close. No, in that moment she looked like the young lady she had been many moons ago, proud and free, with long-flowing hair and eyes of emerald green to break men's hearts.

Why, I never knewed she was such a beauter, thought Polly. *It's breath-takin', that's what!*

'**Be gone!**' cried Old Granny again, advancing on Mr Gum and Billy. '**Be gone, foul stinkers of the night, and** – oh,' she whimpered, falling to the floor as her knee gave way like old people's knees sometimes do. And with that, Old Granny was a wrinkler once more and her commanding was done.

'Looks like your sherry just ran out, you interferin' peppercorn,' laughed Mr Gum, kicking the empty bottle from her hand. 'Now, come on,

Billy me boy,' he growled, throwing open the front door and pushing Polly out into the rainy night. 'We got evil Destinies to fulfill!'

Chapter 17

Meanwhile, Over in Spain

Meanwhile, Friday O'Leary was sitting on a beach in Spain with his lovely missus – Mrs Lovely. Oh, what a perfect place for a honeymoon it was! The sky was blue and the warm sea was filled with laughing Spanish gypsies and their faithful donkeys. And all the while the President of Spain flew high overhead in his hot-air balloon, dropping doughnuts and toys on to the merrymakers below.

'Mrs Lovely, I'm really glad I married you,' sighed Friday contentedly. 'And I'm not just saying that because you run the sweetshop and I get free stuff.'

'Oh, Friday,' trilled Mrs Lovely. 'You say the most romantic things and that was one of them.'

'Hey, let's get married AGAIN,' said Friday

suddenly. 'Then we'll be DOUBLE-MARRIED and we'll probably be able to read each other's thoughts!'

'O . . . K,' said Mrs Lovely uncertainly – but before Friday could explain further, a small Spanish boy wearing a hat of many colours approached.

'Señor Friday, Señora Mrs Lovely,' said the boy with his honest face. 'I bring bad news from your hometown of Lamonic Bibber. Señorita Polly is in trouble and you must hurry back home!'

'Hold on, young fella-me-lad, don't I know you?' said Friday, narrowing his eyes, for the boy seemed somehow familiar.

'No, Señor Friday,' replied the boy. 'I am just an ordinary Spanish youngster whom you have never seen before in your life. But now I must go! Adiós!' And tossing them a couple of Spanish fruit chews, away he raced.

'That was the Spirit of the Rainbow, I know it!'

Friday told his wife excitedly. 'It was him, it was! He's always doing stuff like that!'

'Never mind that now,' said Mrs Lovely. 'Didn't you hear what the boy said? Polly's in trouble.'

'Then there's no time to lose!' cried Friday. 'Señor Darren!' he called to one of the gypsies. 'Bring me your fastest donkey!'

In a matter of moments, Señor Darren had rounded up the fastest donkey of them all, a graceful brute by the name of Barcelona Jim. Friday and Mrs Lovely jumped on as the donkey waded into the sea. Then Friday attached a powerful speedboat motor to its tail and – **SPLASH!** – off they roared.

'VORSICHT! ES GIBT EINE KLEINE EULE HINTER DIR!' yelled Friday. 'That means "THE TRUTH IS A LEMON MERINGUE!" in Spanish,' he told his wife proudly.*

'Don't worry, Polly, dear! We're coming to

* No it doesn't.

save you!' cried Mrs Lovely as they gunned over the waves, and with that the heroes were on their way.

Chapter 18

Polly Goes Back to the Windmill

'It's no use screamin' for help,' Mr Gum told Polly as Billy William dragged her through the rainy streets of Lamonic Bibber. 'So don't try it again,' he grinned ferociously, leaning so close into Polly's face that she could see every single fly in his beard. 'Not unless you want Billy here to feed you a nice big plate of steamin' cold entrails, that is.'

'An' trotters,' added Billy. 'I just received a new shipment of trotters. Fancy some, do ya?'

'That shut 'er up,' sneered Mr Gum, and on they marched in grim silence. On through the wind and the rain and the cold, past the high street where the shops stood closed, their shutters drawn against the coming storm. On past the railway tracks where Crazy Barry Fungus lived in his silver birdcage.

'Tweet! Tweet! I'm a lovely little chaffinch!'

he called out hopefully. But there was to be no birdseed for Crazy Barry Fungus that evening. Instead, Billy William kicked a load of mud into his face – and on they marched.

Overhead, thunderclouds were moving in, great big purple-black ones like those bruises you sometimes get on bananas or rugby players. The storm was on its way.

Jus' like that storm what done killed Nicholas de Twinklecakes' family, thought Polly with a cold shiver. Was Old Granny right? Was the past repeating itself? Was the past repeating itself? Was the past repeating itself?

And on they marched.

Afterwards, Polly hardly remembered anything of that terrible journey. All she had were vague images – the horrid, churning mud at their feet, Billy tugging at the meaty old rope to hurry her along, hundreds of *Crunchy Little Leopards* floating down the river in a postman's hat, terrified out of their tiny cereal minds . . . Mr Gum laughing as a bolt of lightning got Billy William in the leg, even though he was meant to be Billy's friend . . .

How they made it to the windmill Polly never knew.

But eventually, soaking wet and splattered with mud, there they were, standing before the windmill's dreadful gaze even though it didn't have any eyes. Oh, what a terrifying sight it was. Hideous ravens and crows looped and whirled round its sails, screeching like the Devil's Travelling Bird Circus of Doom. Rats peered out from every nook and cranny, spitting and burping up bits of sick all over the place. And a daddy-long-legs sat cockily on the doorstep as if to say, 'Evil has taken over and I am the new King of the World!' Then a starling ate it.

But worse than any of this were the thunderclouds gathering over the windmill, gathering, yes, gathering themselves into an enormous face. And that face was twisted up with so much anger and hatred that even Mr Gum was impressed.

'GOOD EVENING,' said the terrifying face of clouds, gigantic in the dark skies above. 'GUESS WHAT? I AM NICHOLAS DE TWINKLECAKES! AND I HAVE COME BACK THROUGH TIME TO WATCH AS LAMONIC BIBBER BURNS! PLUS I JUST FANCIED HAVING A LOOK AROUND AT THE 21ST CENTURY. AND IT LOOKS ABSOLUTELY RUBBISH!'

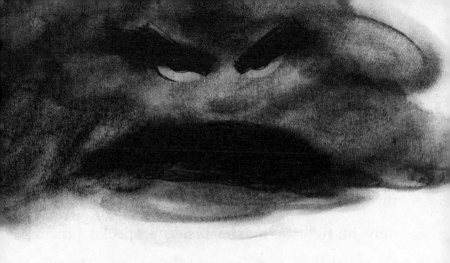

'Well, you're wrong, you insane bundle of clouds!' shouted Polly bravely. 'It's totally brilliant an' we gots the Internet an' stuff, so shut up!'

'NO, *YOU* SHUT UP!' thundered the face, snotting out a massive lightning bolt which Polly only just managed to dodge.

'HA HA HA!' Nicholas' mad laughter boomed

through the Heavens though he himself belonged only in Hell, or maybe inside a special prison for naughty giant faces made of weather. And he was still laughing as Mr Gum and Billy crossed the rickety wooden bridge, dragging Polly along behind them.

At last! whispered the power crystals, glowing bright against the darkness. *We're finally going back to the windmill where we were made!*

'THAT'S RIGHT,' boomed Nicholas de

Twinklecakes. 'THANKS FOR ALL YOUR HELP, MR GUM.'

'No problem, Nick-Nacks, me old trifle,' laughed Mr Gum. 'You don't mind if I call you Nick-Nacks, do you?'

'I DO MIND A LITTLE BIT,' admitted Nicholas. 'PLEASE TRY NOT TO DO IT AGAIN. NOW GO AND MAKE MY AMAZING CURSE COME TRUE!'

'No problem, Nick-Nacks,' grinned Mr Gum. And with that he snurfled through the dark doorway and into the windmill. Billy William snooded in after him, and Polly had no choice but to follow.

Chapter 19
Inside the Windmill

'Whisker me shabbas,' muttered Mr Gum. 'It's dark in here!'

As if in response, the power crystals began to glow with their strange pink and white light, pulsing in and out like a disco for vampires. And in that eerie glow Polly saw the windmill's machinery, full of cogs and wheels and cruel sharp metal teeth that would slice and dice and splice whatever came their way. She shivered to think of its awful power.

Jus' a-lyin' in wait 'til it starts up again, she thought. *Like a Godzilla what's only pretendin' to be dead but when you poke it with a spoon it quickly springs up an' munches your face off.*

Beyond the machinery rose a flight of rotten

wooden stairs, disappearing into the darkness above. And now, holding the crystals before them like a torch, the villains began to climb.

CLURP. CLURP. CLURP.

Up those stairs they clurped in their hobnail boots and once more Polly had no choice but to follow, the rubbery intestine rope cutting into her wrists all the while.

'Forces of Good,' she prayed under her breath, 'It's Polly here. I hopes you're well.

Thanks for last weekend when I found that pound coin in the park. Anyway, listen, right? If ever I did needed a miracle it's now, so won't you sends help?'

'Will this do?' whispered a voice from above and Polly felt a small weight land on her right shoulder, almost causing her to cry out. But suddenly she realised – it was her good friend Alan Taylor, the gingerbread headmaster with electric muscles!

'A.T., is it really you?' she replied as softly as she could.

'Yes, Polly,' he whispered. 'Old Granny told me what was happening. I've been hiding in the rafters waiting for you to arrive. Now hold still.'

And bravely little Alan Taylor nibbled through the rope of intestines that bound Polly, even though he had recently turned vegetarian for religious reasons.

'There,' he whispered. 'You're free.'

'What's that whisperin'?' cried Mr Gum suddenly, spinning around fast as a toffee apple. But Alan Taylor was faster still, and quickly he hid in Polly's hair.

'Why, it's only the wind a-howlin',' explained Polly. 'Sometimes it sounds jus' like Alan Taylor, I've often noticed. But Alan Taylor himself is probbly miles away teachin' his pupils all 'bout the natural world.'

'Well, he better be,' snapped Mr Gum, with a vicious gnash of his teeth. 'If I see that little tungler 'round here I'll scoff him up once an' for all.'

By now the criminals had reached the small room at the very top of the windmill. And there it sat – the Power Crystal Control Panel that Nicholas de Twinklecakes had made out of floorboards all those years ago. On the top were two slots, exactly the right shape and size for the power crystals. But which crystal went in which slot? It didn't say.

'How does this blibberin' thing work?' snarled Mr Gum in frustration. 'I ain't got time for no riddles from the past!'

'Oi, Nick-Nacks!' yelled Billy, sticking his

head out of the window into the dark night sky. 'Which way round do them crystals go?'

'I CAN'T REMEMBER,' shrugged Nicholas. 'I HAVE BEEN DEAD FOR NEARLY FIVE HUNDRED YEARS, YOU KNOW.'

While the villains were distracted, Alan Taylor was busy fastening on a brand new pair of goggles for his traditional 'jump-at-the-baddies' bit. He loved jumping at the baddies and who could blame him? He was absolutely superb at it.

Yet even while he fastened his goggles he was busy teaching Polly about the natural world he loved so much.

'Many animals make their home inside windmills,' he explained. 'For instance, that small white thing in the corner is known as a "mouse". And that small grey thing next to it is known as "some fluff". But now to business,' he whispered. His goggles were ready at last.

'GINGERBREAD, GINGERBREAD, RAH-RAH-RAH!'

And so saying, Alan Taylor launched himself from Polly's shoulder straight for his number one target.

'TAYLOR!' roared Mr Gum in pain as the fearless biscuit bit into his big wibbling nose. The villain's hands flew to his face and the power crystals dropped from his clutches, falling to the floor with a hollow clinking sound.

For a moment everyone just stood there as they took in what had happened. Then suddenly they all dived at once.

'Got one!' cried Polly, grabbing hold of the white crystal as she skidded wildly over the smooth wooden floor.

'Got one!' shouted Billy, slurping up the pink crystal with his long grey tongue. In a smelly flash Billy ran over to the Control Panel and dribbled the crystal into one of the slots. But was it the right slot?

CLANK! GRRRRUUURK! FRROINKLE! BRP.

Slowly the windmill's cruel sharp machinery cranked up.

'GOOD GUESS, BUTCHER GUY!' cried Nicholas de Twinklecakes' enormo-face from outside the window. 'NOW PUT THE OTHER ONE IN, SMALL GIRL!'

'No way, you historical roo-de-lally!' shot back Polly. 'I'm not doin' your dirty works!'

'RAAARRRGGH!' roared Nicholas. 'THEN FACE THE MIGHTY FURY OF MY FURIOUS MIGHTY FACE!', and once more he did lightning bolts out his nose, it was horrible.

FIZZ! FIZZ! DODGE!

Polly leapt round the room, dodging those bad zappers for her very life, but Nicholas had other tricks up his face. Suddenly he puffed out those colossal thundercloud cheeks of his and **SPLURP!** He spat a big jet of rain right at Polly, knocking the white crystal from her hand.

Up towards the ceiling the crystal flew, spinning, spinning, end over end – and then all at once, down it plummeted, straight towards the empty slot in the Control Panel.

Yes! laughed the white crystal gleefully as it fell. *Time to fulfil my evil Destiny at last!*

'NO!' cried Alan Taylor, and with all his electric muscles whirring he leapt desperately from Mr Gum's nose towards the misbehaving crystal.

Biscuit-Punch!

He smashed it away with his gingerbread hand, and in that moment Alan Taylor was the true King Of Heroes you've ever seen or heard about on TV, for he had saved the whole of Lamonic Bibber from going up in flames. No two ways about it, it was his best jump ever.

But was it also to be his last? The next moment Alan Taylor was hurtling towards the slot himself, his juicy raisin eyes wide with fear.

'Polly!' he gasped. 'See that thing with six legs crawling on the wall? It is known as a "beetl–'

But his words were lost as he fell into the slot and was swallowed up in the grinding machinery below. All those cogs and wheels and cruel metal teeth. A spray of biscuit crumbs went up, his electric muscles whirred one last time . . .

And that was the end of little Alan Taylor, a teacher of the natural world till his dying breath.

Alan crumbs
↓

Chapter 20

Midsummer's Eve

For a moment Polly just stood there in disbelief. Alan Taylor? Gone? After all they'd been through together? It couldn't be true.

All those times they'd sat together on Boaster's Hill watching the clouds drift by.

All those times they'd played chess and he

secretly always let Polly win.

The time when that stray cat gobbled up one of his eyes and Polly got him a new one from the kitchen cupboard. How they had laughed!

There would be no more of those times ever again.

🐱 🐱 🐱

'NOW YOU HAVE LEARNED THE SAME LESSON I DID, LITTLE GIRL!' laughed Nicholas de

Twinklecakes from outside. 'LIFE IS COMPLETELY UNFAIR AND SO YOU MUST GO EVIL! JUST LIKE ME!'

Polly knew that there was no truth in Nicholas' bitter words. But she was sick with grief and anger and for the first time ever, the Bad Side was risin', risin', risin' up inside her nine-year-old heart.

'Now hang on just a minute, Bad Side,' said the

Forces of Good inside Polly's heart. 'Don't you know whose heart this is? It is Polly's and it is pure and brave and true. You can't just come risin', risin', risin' up in here, you know!'

'Well, bad luck, cos we're a-gonna anyway,' laughed the Bad Side. And without further ado the Bad Side did an enormous wee all over the Forces of Good and kicked them over a cliff.

For the first time ever, the Bad Side of Polly's heart had won the day.

'I hates everythin' now!' shouted Polly angrily, snatching up the white power crystal. 'I been a-driven mad by grief an' now I'm a-gonna finish the job of destroyin' this rotten town my very self!'

'That's it, little girl,' grinned Mr Gum. 'Come over to the Bad Side.'

'Yeah,' said Billy William, a load of entrails hanging from his mouth. 'Be like us!'

'YEAH!' said Nicholas de Twinklecakes. He

couldn't really think of anything else to add so he just did a bit of lightning and impressive hovering about to remind everyone how frightening he was.

The storm smashed and crashed against the windmill, shaking it to the very foundations. But Polly's hand was steady as she prepared to slot the crystal into the Control Panel.

'I hates it all!' she sobbed. 'I am gonna do it, I swears it!'

'That's right,' said Mr Gum. 'Fill your heart

with evil, like a cruel dustman eating spaghetti in front of starvin' puppies.'

'I will,' said Polly in a voice she hardly recognised as her own. And slowly, as the storm raged and the light flickered madly inside the room, Polly lowered the white power crystal towards the slot.

But the Forces of Good weren't giving up just yet. For so long as there are laughing children in the world, and hilarious cartoons on

TV, and snowball fights, and brilliant pop music with tremendous choruses, the Forces of Good will rise once more and the Bad Side hasn't got a chance.

And now, as Polly lowered that crystal, her angry hand it did pause. For what was that outrageous racket coming from outside? Was it – could it be – yes, it was!

It was the barking of a massive whopper of a dog and the braying of a magnificent donkey. And never had two animal's noises sounded so heroic. The incredible sounds flew into Polly's ears and crammed her head with joy and she fell to her knees as the Forces of Good rushed back into her heart where they belonged.

'You bunch of CUCUMBERS!' she yelled at the villains. 'I'm not NEVER gonna go evil, so shut, I said, shut, I said SHUT RIGHT UP!'

'Shabba me WHISKERS!' Mr Gum shouted furiously. 'What a bother it all is!'

And before Polly knew what was what, Mr Gum had snatched the white crystal from her grasp and slammed it into the Control Panel as hard as you like.

ZRRRRRA·Ck! A flash of pink-white light ripped across the sky as the power of the crystals was unleashed.

THWWWWACK! The heavens rolled with unnatural thunder and fury. **WHIIIIIRRRRRRRRRRRR!** The noise of the machinery rose louder and louder against the crashing storm.

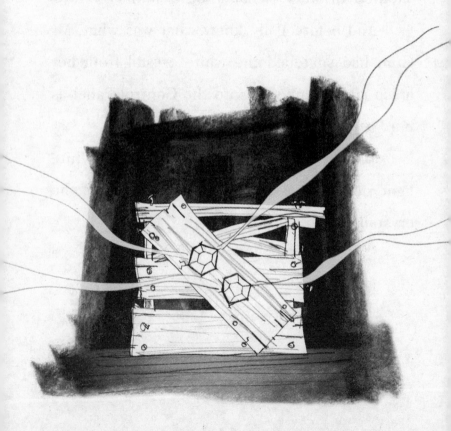

For the first time in centuries, the windmill's sails were about to turn.

'We done it, we done it!' shouted Mr Gum and Billy, dancing round and round the room, their dirty shadows bobbing crazily over the walls as the lightning flashed outside.

'Come on, Billy me boy,' cried Mr Gum. 'Let's go an' drink loads of beer an' watch the town burnin' down on TV! See ya later, Nick-Nacks!'

And with that, the pair of them were gone from the windmill and running off into the dark stormy night, racing away over the flooded fields and meadows like the cowards they were.

Slowly, in a daze, Polly looked around her. The last few minutes had been so confusing. What had happened? Why was she in the windmill? What was it all about? She could hardly even remember her own name. She thought it might be Dorothy Epstein.

'Polly! Polly! Are you all right?' cried an anxious voice from outside, and stumbling over to the window Polly saw a wonderful sight. It was Friday O'Leary together with Mrs Lovely. They were sitting on a Spanish donkey and yes, Jake the dog was there too, splashing around in the raindrops for the pure fun of it.

And now it all came flooding back and Polly knew who she was and what it was she had to do.

'Listen!' she yelled down to her friends. 'Like the curse does say,

'When next the windmill's sails do turn, Lamonic Bibber will burn and burn!

'So we gots to stop the sails turnin'!' she

pleaded. 'It's our only hope!'

'Never you worry, little miss!' shouted Friday, producing a really long rope from under his hat. 'How can we fail? We've got a really long rope!'

He tossed it up into the sky and how right he was. It wasn't just a really long rope, it was a *really* long rope and it easily made it to the windmill, no problem. Polly caught the end of it and without hesitating she jumped from the window on to the heavy wooden sail beyond.

Lawdy Miss Clawdy, that sail was a slip-slidey old monster! The rain lashed and the wind blew like a xylophone and Nicholas de Twinklecakes kept gobbing bad weather towards Polly and I don't think it was an accident either. He was trying to knock her off, that's what I think. And all the while the sails were turning, faster and faster until Polly was quite certain she'd fall, just like that unlucky egg in the children's nursery rhyme, *Yolk Boy, Yolk Boy, That*

Wall's Not Safe!

But somehow Polly didn't fall. No, somehow she clung on, and soon she had the rope fastened tightly to the sail.

'Quick, Mrs L!' cried Polly, and down on the ground Mrs Lovely threw her end of the rope to the animals. Instantly they grabbed it up between their teeth, all three of them – Jake, Barcelona Jim and Friday O'Leary.

'Now PULL!' Mrs Lovely commanded the

mighty beasts. 'PULL, I say!'

And pull they did, like no beasts have ever
pulled before or since. With all their might they

pulled, the sweat running down their faces, the muscles on their necks standing out with the strain.

But even as they struggled, the sails made their first complete turn and Polly saw a lick of flame spring up in the distance, a lick of flame as tall as a hotel. The power crystals were doing their terrible work and Lamonic Bibber was about to burn.

'For the Forces of Good – PULL HARDER!' commanded Mrs Lovely and Polly together.

'WOOF!' barked Jake, digging his paws deeper still into the muddy ground.

'HEE-HAW!' brayed Barcelona Jim, grimacing as he tugged on the rope.

'NEIGH!' bellowed Friday, tossing back his head wildly. 'NEEEEIIIIIGGGGHH!'

'You've nearly done it!' shouted Polly. 'The sails are a-slowin'! Keep pullin', keep pullin'!'

'But how much longer can they pull?' cried Mrs Lovely anxiously. For the brave beasts were almost at the end of their strength.

'Hang on!' shouted Polly suddenly. 'Try tyin'

the rope to that enormous castle over there! That oughts to hold it!'

It's true, there was a massive castle next door to the windmill, I forgot to mention it before. And a pyramid.

Panting and heaving, inch by hairy inch, the tiring beasts dragged that rope towards the castle. And Mrs Lovely ran over and with her nimble little hands she tied the end of the rope to the castle's door.

And then and only then, the windmill's sails
came
to
a
complete
stop.

o o o

And so it was done. In the wind and the rain and the howling of the storm, the sails of the windmill stood still once more. With the last of her strength Polly slid down the rope and crawled over to where the great beasts lay in an exhausted heap, their sides moving rapidly in and out as they recovered from their ordeal. Mrs Lovely sat beside the poor things, patting and stroking and making soothing noises all the while.

'There, there, boy,' she said, popping a sugar lump into Friday's quivering mouth. 'There,

there, it's all right now.'

'Mrs – Lovely,' gasped Polly. 'Mrs – Lovely, is – it – really – over?'

'Yes,' came a voice just then. 'The terror is truly at an end.'

And standing at the window of the windmill, gazing out peacefully over them all was none other than that wondrous boy, the Spirit of the Rainbow.

'Friends,' he beamed. 'You have all worked hard together to save the day and the Forces of

Good are very proud of you. But now your work is done. It is my turn to shine.'

Without another word, the honest lad removed the power crystals from the Control Panel. At once the flames in the distance disappeared and Lamonic Bibber was safe and sound.

'We don't need this any longer,' said the boy, cutting the rope from the windmill's sail with his special Rainbow Scissors. 'It's time to make the world glow with happy colours once more.'

And then the Spirit of the Rainbow did a very strange thing. He took the power crystals and put them back into the Control Panel,

I'm not even kidding, he really really did.

'Spirit of the Rainbow, DON'T!' cried Polly in horror. 'You're gonna make it all start up 'gain!'

'Yes, child,' nodded the boy, though he was no older than she. 'But look! I have put the pink crystal in the white slot – and the white crystal in the pink slot. You see, Nicholas de Twinklecakes designed the power crystals to do evil.'

'IT'S TRUE,' admitted Nicholas from up in the sky. 'SORRY ABOUT THAT, EVERYONE.'

'But by reversing the crystals,' continued the boy, 'they will now do *good* deeds instead. From this day forth the windmill will be on our side, and it will make delicious loaves of bread for all!'

'A wop bop-a-lu bop, a wop bam boom!' shouted everyone happily.

And from where she sat, Polly saw something

that everybody else had missed. It was Nicholas de Twinklecakes again. He was still made out of clouds, but he was no longer an evil madman. No, he was a handsome young man indeed, with the merriest smile Polly had ever seen.

On either side of him stood his wife and son. They too were made out of clouds, with happy bluebirds perching on their eyebrows and smiles so dazzling that Polly had to put on sunglasses just to look at them.

'Thank you, Polly,' said Nicholas de Twinklecakes in a gentle voice like a soft summer breeze. 'You and your pals are the best.'

'Hoorah,' said his wife and son. 'Hoorah hoorah hoorah.'

'Now come on,' said Nicholas, turning towards his beautiful dead family of ghosts. 'Let's go to Heaven and play table tennis forever and ever and ever, or even longer if possible.'

And as the reunited de Twinklecakes drifted

away to that magical place, the rain stopped falling and the storm clouds disappeared. And the moon rose peacefully in the evening sky, humming a jazzy melody on its silvery breath. It was going to be a beautiful night.

But Alan Taylor isn't here to see it, remembered Polly all of a sudden. And though the battle was won, her heart was filled with sorrow.

Chapter 21
Captain Excellent

'**A** shes to ashes,' said Friday. 'Crumbs to crumbs.'

The heroes stood beneath a starry sky in the Old Meadow yonder, down by the Lamonic River where the water rushes grow. They were burying their good friend, Alan Taylor.

Well, actually they were burying a small drawing of him done by Polly especially for the occasion. It was all they had to remember him by.

Gently Friday laid the drawing in a hole in the ground and together, Jake and Barcelona Jim covered it over with earth.

''Tis a sad night,' said Old Granny, who had come down to the meadow when she heard the news. 'Aye, 'tis a sad, sad night,' she said again, weeping into her handkerchief and having a crafty sip of sherry at the same time.

'Very true,' said Friday, gazing off into the distance. 'But life is life and death is death and Alan Taylor will never be forgotten. THE TRUTH IS A LEMON MERINGUE! He was the best biscuit I ever knew. For a start, he was the only one who could talk and run around and ride a little toy bicycle.'

'He done taught me so much 'bout the natural world,' sniffed Polly. 'He knew all the names of all the creatures, no matter how great nor snail.'

'And though he himself was small, he was a true giant among men,' nodded Friday, 'and I hereby award him the highest title possible – the title of Captain Excellent. Thank you, Captain

Excellent, wherever you are!'

'Yes, thank you, Captain Excellent!' echoed the others. And for a long while everyone sat there in silence, remembering their friend.

'But come,' said the Spirit of the Rainbow at last, as dawn was breaking over the horizon. 'Today is a new day and just as the sun rises, so too do delicious loaves of bread. Let us feast together.'

Wearily the others followed the lad over to

the windmill. They watched unenthusiastically as he started up the machinery. No one really felt like breakfast but presently an early morning breeze caught the windmill's sails. And soon enough, a fresh loaf of bread appeared on the conveyor belt, the first loaf of bread the windmill had made since Nicholas de Twinklecakes' time. Only it wasn't a loaf of bread at all, it was a different kind of baked good altogether. In fact –

'It's a gingerbread man,' gasped Old Granny.

'With electric muscles!' cried Polly.

'Could it be –' wondered Mrs Lovely.

'Woof?' said Jake.

'THE TRUTH IS A LEMON MERINGUE!' shouted Friday. 'It's Captain Excellent!'

'Otherwise known as Alan Taylor!' laughed Polly in delight. 'He's been baked again! Alan Taylor! Alan Taylor, you're back at Number 1 on the Not Bein' Dead Charts an' that's a official Polly fact! Spirit of the Rainbow, how did you knows?'

But the Spirit of the Rainbow had gone and where he had stood there were only a couple of fruit chews glistening sweetly among the dewdrops.

'Never mind him now!' laughed Alan Taylor, jumping up to kiss Polly on the nose. 'It IS me!

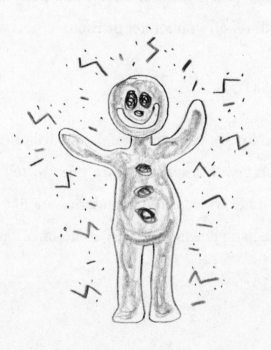

What an adventure, Polly! What strange things I saw while I was dead! They only added to my knowledge of the natural world, and perhaps one day I will teach you all about them.'

And who knows? Perhaps one day he will. But until then, there will be plenty more tales to tell about Polly and her friends. You see, stories are like rivers – they keep on flowing and they sometimes have fish in them. And just as sure as the river flows, there will always be another adventure rolling around the bend. For as Old Granny said that fine summer's morn, as everyone sat laughing in the sunshine,

The past has a way of repeating itself.

The past has a way of repeating itself.

The past has a way of repeating itself.

But the future? Well, now, that's another story.

THE END

THE BALLAD OF BARRY FUNGUS
Words and music: Friday O'Leary

Barry was a fine young man
When he went off to war
With a hi-ho-diddle and a hi-ho-dee!
And a rifle sitting on his knee
And a flask filled with his grandma's tea
Crazy Barry Fungus

He shot one hundred soldiers down
His very first day at war
With a hi-ho-diddle and a hi-ho-dee!
Bang-bang! He shot 'em, one two three!
'The soldier's life is the life for me!'
Said Crazy Barry Fungus

The general took him to one side
And punched him in the neck
With a hi-ho-diddle and a hi-ho-dee!
The general said, 'What's wrong with thee?
You're meant to shoot the enemy!
You stupid dangerous weirdo.'

They sent him home that very day
In absolute disgrace
With a hi-ho-diddle and a hi-ho-dee!
Ignored by friends and family
They were too ashamed to want to see
Crazy Barry Fungus

He went to live by the railway tracks
In a gilded silver cage
With a hi-ho-diddle and a hi-ho-dee!
'A man I don't deserve to be,
I'll be a chaffinch, tweety-twee!'
Chirped Crazy Barry Fungus

And ever since that day, my friends
A chaffinch he has been
With a hi-ho-diddle and a hi-ho-dee!
He flaps in his cage and begs for seed
He'd like to leave but he's lost the key
Crazy Barry Fungus

So if you chance to see him
Upon a rainy night
With a high-ho-diddle and a hi-ho-dee!
Please be kind, give gen'rously
For one day you might be like he –
Living in a birdcage

(Four hour long harmonica solo)

FIN

About the Author

Andy Stanton lives in North London. He studied English at Oxford but they kicked him out. He has been a film script reader, a cartoonist, an NHS lackey and lots of other things. He has many interests, but best of all he likes cartoons, books and music (even jazz). One day he'd like to live in New York or Berlin or one of those places because he's got fantasies of bohemia. His favourite expression is 'I like straws' and his favourite word is 'upstart'. This is his seventh book.

About the Illustrator

David Tazzyman lives in South London with his girlfriend, Melanie, and their son, Stanley. He grew up in Leicester, studied illustration at Manchester Metropolitan University and then travelled around Asia for three years before moving to London in 1997. He likes football, cricket, biscuits, music and drawing. He still dislikes celery.

Have you read all the

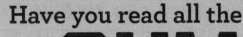

MR GUM

books?

They're WELL BRILLIANT!

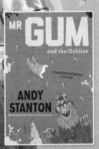

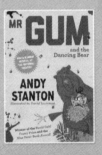

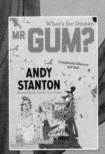

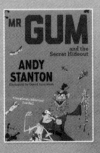

THOUGHT **MR GUM** WAS WEIRD?
WELL, JUST WAIT TIL YOU MEET . . .

THE PANINIS

OF POMPEII

VESUVIUS →

CAECILIUS

DON'T ASK

SLAVIUS

A FROG

BARKUS
WOOFERINICUM

FELIUS

ANOTHER FROG

More mind-bending craziness from

ANDY STANTON

Illustrated by Sholto Walker

IT'S
TOGA-LLY
TERRIFIC!